THIS IS
DOCTOR STRANGE

Adapted by Alexandra West

Illustrated by Simone Di Meo, Mario Del Pennino, *and* Tommaso Moscardini

Based on the Marvel comic book series Doctor Strange

ABDO
Spotlight

MARVEL

Los Angeles
New York

ABDOPUBLISHING.COM

Reinforced library bound edition published in 2018 by Spotlight, a division of ABDO,
PO Box 398166, Minneapolis, Minnesota 55439. Spotlight produces high-quality
reinforced library bound editions for schools and libraries. Published by Marvel Press,
an imprint of Disney Book Group.

Printed in the United States of America, North Mankato, Minnesota.
042017
092017

THIS BOOK CONTAINS
RECYCLED MATERIALS

marvelkids.com

© 2016 MARVEL

PUBLISHER'S CATALOGING-IN-PUBLICATION DATA

Names: West, Alexandra, author. | Di Meo, Simone ; Del Pennino, Mario ; Moscardini,
  Tommaso, illustrators.
Title: Doctor Strange: this is Doctor Strange / writer: Alexandra West ; art: Simone Di
  Meo ; Mario Del Pennino ; Tommaso Moscardini.
Other titles: This is Doctor Strange
Description: Reinforced library bound edition. | Minneapolis, Minnesota : Spotlight,
  2018. | Series: World of reading level 1
Summary: Discover how former surgeon Stephen Strange became the magical Doctor
  Strange.
Identifiers: LCCN 2017936170 | ISBN 9781532140570 (lib. bdg.)
Subjects: LCSH: Superheroes--Juvenile fiction. | Comic books, strips, etc.--Juvenile
  fiction. | Graphic novels--Juvenile fiction.
Classification: DDC [Fic]--dc23
LC record available at https://lccn.loc.gov/2017936170

Spotlight

A Division of ABDO
abdopublishing.com

This is Stephen Strange.

Stephen is also Doctor Strange.
Doctor Strange is a Super Hero!

Stephen was not always
Doctor Strange.
He was once a surgeon.

Surgeons use their hands to help people.
Stephen's hands were strong and steady.

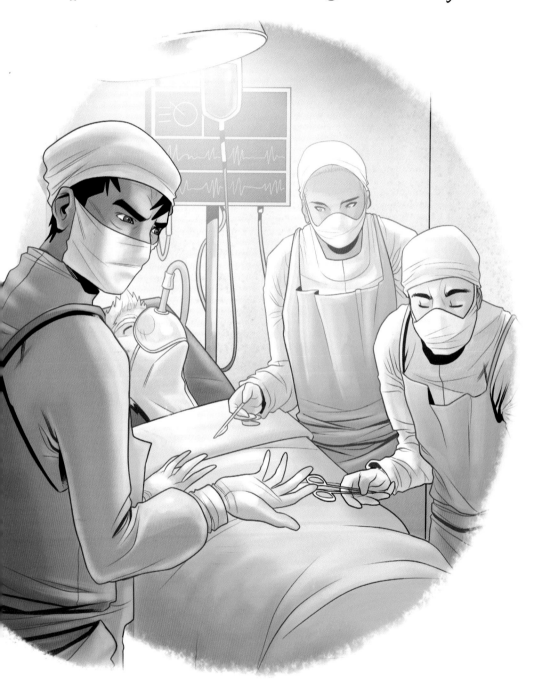

Stephen liked what he did.
He made people feel better.

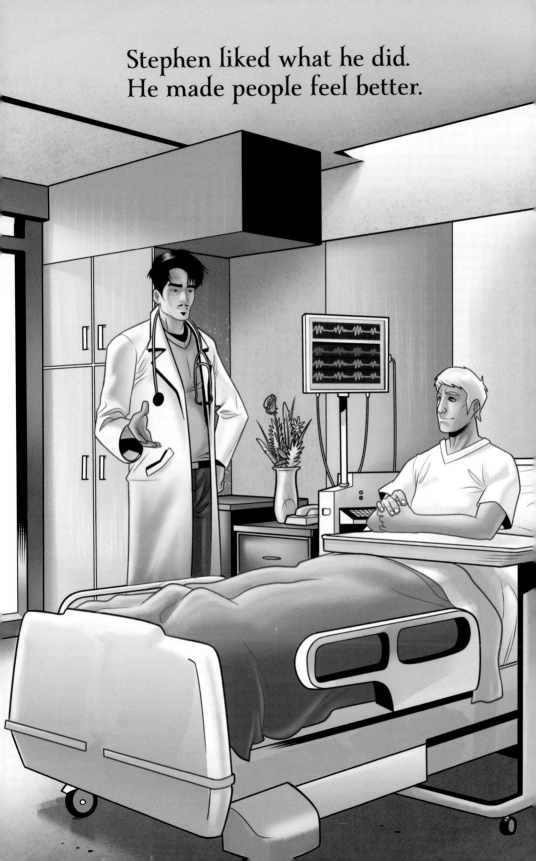

One day, Stephen was in an accident.
His hands were hurt.
Stephen was told his hands would
never get better.
That made Stephen sad.

Stephen needed to fix his hands.
He went away for help.
He went to another country.

A man told Stephen about magic.
Magic would fix his hands.
He would find magic in Tibet.

Stephen arrived in Tibet.
Stephen saw someone
being attacked.

Stephen had to
protect the man.

Stephen scared away the thugs.
Stephen saved the man.

The man Stephen helped was called the Ancient One. The Ancient One was thankful. He decided to help Stephen.

Stephen started his training in magic.
Stephen worked hard.
He felt the magic healing his hands.

Stephen became very good at magic!
Stephen became Doctor Strange!

Doctor Strange lives in New York City.

Doctor Strange is a
master of the mystic arts.

Doctor Strange is always busy.
People near and far ask for his help.

They know Doctor Strange
will save them.

Doctor Strange can float.

Doctor Strange has many magical tools.
His tools help him fight the bad guys!

Doctor Strange
uses spell books.
He uses a book
of good spells.

Doctor Strange casts spells.
Doctor Strange saves people
from danger.

Doctor Strange has a magical charm.
The charm has many powers.

It can help Doctor Strange see through illusions.

Doctor Strange has a best friend.
His name is Wong.

Wong teaches Doctor
Strange how to fight.

Doctor Strange fights Super Villains.
He protects the planet from evil!

Doctor Strange has lots
of powerful friends.

Together they fight bad guys.
They make a great team.

Doctor Strange
helps save the day!

Doctor Strange
is a hero!